# Howling at the Hauntlys'

# Howling at the Hauntlys'

by **Marcia Thornton Jones**
and
**Debbie Dadey**

illustrated by **John Steven Gurney**

---

A
**LITTLE APPLE**
PAPERBACK

---

**SCHOLASTIC INC.**
New York   Toronto   London   Auckland   Sydney

*To the howling readers at Dixie,*
*Mary Todd, Johnson, Russell, Harrison, and*
*Picadome Schools in Lexington, KY.—MTJ*

*For my brother, David Wayne Gibson, who is*
*definitely not a werewolf, but has been known*
*to howl at the moon.—DD*

ISBN 0-590-10845-X

Text copyright © 1998 by Marcia Thornton Jones and Debra S. Dadey.
Illustrations copyright © 1998 by Scholastic Inc.
All rights reserved. Published by Scholastic Inc.
LITTLE APPLE PAPERBACKS is a trademark of Scholastic Inc.
THE BAILEY CITY MONSTERS in design is a
trademark of Scholastic Inc.

12 11 10 9 8 7 6 5 4 3                    8 9/9 0 1 2 3/0

Printed in the U.S.A.                                    40

First Scholastic printing, February 1998

Book design by Laurie Williams

# Contents

# 1

## Howling

"That looks silly," Ben told his little sister, Annie.

Annie finished making a raisin smile below her snowman's carrot nose and walnut eyes. "This is what a snowman should look like," she said.

Ben laughed. "Your snowman has no personality. You should make one like mine."

Annie looked at her brother's two-headed snowman. One head had a giant eye in the middle. The other head looked like it was screaming. "Your snowman belongs next door," Annie told him.

Ben and Annie looked at the big house next to theirs. A few months ago, the house had been brand-new. Then the Hauntly family moved in. Now, a loose shutter swayed in the cold wind and most of the windows

had jagged cracks. A lopsided sign hung in the front yard under a dead tree. It said: HAUNTLY MANOR INN. Hauntly Manor looked like something out of a horror movie, and so did the Hauntlys.

Boris Hauntly had slime-green eyes and pointy eyeteeth. He was a dead ringer for Dracula's cousin. His wife, Hilda, always wore a white lab coat covered with strange stains. In fact, Ben and Annie were sure their new neighbors were monsters from Transylvania.

Annie pulled her coat tight. "You know, I think there might be a guest staying at the inn."

"Don't be silly, slush brains." Ben laughed. "There hasn't been a single visitor since the Hauntlys moved in."

"Didn't you hear that howling last night?" Annie asked. "It came from the Hauntlys' backyard."

Ben didn't answer Annie because the door to Hauntly Manor Inn swung open and Kilmer Hauntly stepped out on the porch.

Kilmer was in Ben's class at school, but Kilmer was not a regular fourth-grader. He was very tall, so tall his torn jeans didn't reach all the way to his ankles. Kilmer's hair was cut flat across the top of his head, and he reminded Annie of Frankenstein's monster.

Just before Kilmer closed the front door of Hauntly Manor Inn, his cat, Sparky, darted between his legs. Sparky's black fur went in every direction and she looked like she drank coffee instead of milk. She jumped up on the porch railing. As soon as she saw Annie and Ben, Sparky arched her back and hissed. She leaped off the porch and darted around the corner of the house.

Kilmer waved to Annie and Ben then kicked through the snow until he stood in front of Ben's snowman. "What is this?" Kilmer asked.

Ben patted his two-headed snowman's belly. "This is my newest creation," he said. "Annie thinks it looks like a monster."

Kilmer studied the snowman and finally shook his head. "No, I do not know anyone

4

who looks like that. But it is a fine-looking snowman."

"That's what I think," Ben said with a laugh. "Annie is just crazy."

"I am not," Annie argued.

"Yes, you are," Ben told her. Then he rolled his eyes and looked at Kilmer. "She even thought she heard weird noises coming from your backyard last night."

Kilmer shook his head. "I heard nothing unusual."

"Of course not," Ben said, "because the only unusual nutcase on Dedman Street is Annie."

Annie narrowed her eyes. "You better take that back," she said. "Or else."

"Or else what?" Ben asked, his hands on his hips. Annie didn't answer because just then a snowball smacked Ben on the back of his head.

"Bingo!" Jane yelled. Jane lived down the street and was in the same class as Ben and Kilmer.

"You've done it now," Ben yelled. "This is war. Snowball war!"

Before Ben could throw a snowball at Jane, Annie grabbed his arm. "Shh," she warned. "I hear something."

Ben pulled his arm away. "That old trick isn't going to work. You're just trying to give Jane time to run."

"No, I'm not," Annie said. "I really do hear something very strange."

"I hear it, too," Jane said. "It sounds like it's coming from Kilmer's backyard."

The three kids looked at Kilmer. Kilmer shook his head. "I hear nothing unusual," he said.

Ben stood very still so he could listen. "Wait," he said. "The girls might be right."

"Maybe Sparky is in trouble," Annie said.

"There's only one way to find out," Ben said. Without waiting for his friends, Ben took off running toward the back of Hauntly Manor Inn. What he found was hairy, but it was definitely not a cat.

# 2

## Cousin Hauntly

When Kilmer, Annie, and Jane rounded the corner of Hauntly Manor, they found a huge hairy creature pawing through the snow near the screened-in porch. If he hadn't been wearing torn jeans and an old plaid shirt, Jane would've been sure that he was a giant wolf burying a bone.

Kilmer smiled. "It is just my cousin," he told Annie, Ben, and Jane. "His nickname is Fang. He flew in from Transylvania yesterday. He is Hauntly Manor Inn's first guest." Kilmer patted his cousin on the back.

When Kilmer's cousin faced them, Jane gasped and Annie took a giant step back.

Kilmer was different-looking, but the kids were used to him. They weren't used to Fang, though. Fang stood a full head taller than Kilmer and was several years

older. Fang was the hairiest kid they had ever seen. He had thick brown hair that came down to a point on his forehead, but that wasn't all. He also had hair on his knuckles and Annie noticed hair peeking out from under his shirtsleeves. There was even hair sticking out from under his jeans and all over his bare feet.

Fang smiled, showing his long yellow canine teeth. "I am happy to meet Kilmer's friends," he said. His voice was rough and sounded like growling.

"We heard something," Annie said. "We thought Sparky might be in trouble."

For a minute, Jane was sure Fang snarled. Then he laughed, only it didn't sound like laughing. It sounded like howling. "I didn't see Kilmer's cat. Believe me, you'd know if I did." Fang licked his lips. "I'd be glad to hunt for the cat. There's not much else to do around here."

Ben grinned. "How about having a snowball fight?" he suggested. "Boys against girls?"

10

Annie held up her hand. "That's not fair. There are more boys than girls."

Ben nodded. "I know. Before Kilmer moved to Dedman Street, I was always outnumbered. It's about time the boys had the advantage."

"Two girls can beat three boys any day of the week," Jane said as she launched a handful of snow at Ben's face.

Ben ran for a big pile of snow. "War!" he yelled to Kilmer and Fang.

Kilmer and Ben threw dozens of snowballs at the girls, but Fang was a machine. He jumped down in the snow and quickly scratched up dozens of balls. He hopped up and pelted the girls with the balls. Every time Fang made a direct hit, he would tilt his head back to howl in delight. Fang howled a lot. It gave Annie the chills.

There was no way Annie and Jane could make snowballs fast enough. It looked like they were doomed to lose the snowball war. Just as Jane was ready to call a truce, a snowball sailed over her and landed right

on Kilmer's flat head. Another snowball smacked Ben on the arm. Three more snowballs sailed at the boys like missiles on a battlefield.

"Look out!" Ben yelled. "It's an invasion!"

# 3

# Monster Attack

Kilmer's parents, Boris and Hilda, swooped up beside Annie and Jane. "How about a little help?" Boris asked.

Jane nodded while Hilda launched a snowball right into Ben's head. Boris smiled, showing his pointy eyeteeth, and tossed a ball toward Fang. Annie shivered a bit when she saw Boris' teeth, but she forgot all about it when they started winning the snowball fight.

"Your parents are smearing us!" Ben yelled to Kilmer. Ever since Boris and Hilda joined the fight, the boys were getting hit from the left and right. "I've never seen parents get into a snowball fight like your parents," Ben said.

Kilmer smiled. "I know. Aren't they great?"

"There's nothing great about losing," Ben grumbled.

Fang didn't say anything. He was busy launching three snowballs at once. One hit Boris on the shoulder. Fang tilted his head back and howled.

Kilmer ducked when another snowball whizzed by his cheek. "We were beating the girls. They needed the help."

"It's not fair," Ben said. "Your mom and dad are helping them mash us into slush." Ben quickly launched a snowball toward Jane. Kilmer threw one, too.

Jane dodged the snowball and it hit Kilmer's mom instead. Hilda threw back her head of wild hair and laughed. She looked at Boris and smiled. "This is wonderful. I wish we could have snow every day of the year."

Boris smiled, showing his pointy eye-teeth. His slime-green eyes flashed as he tossed his long black cape onto the ground. "Enjoy it while you can, my dear," Boris said. "It soon will melt."

15

Hilda nodded at Boris and didn't notice Fang's snowball coming straight for her. BLAM! The snowball hit her right in the mouth.

"That's it for me!" Hilda shouted.

Ben, Kilmer, and Fang ran up to Hilda. "Aunt Hilda, are you all right?" Fang asked.

Hilda nodded and brushed the snow off her pale face. "I am fine," Hilda said to the kids, "but I imagine you are getting hungry. How about a rare calves' liver treat?"

"Bloody good!" Fang yelled, licking his lips.

Annie's stomach did a flip-flop and Jane shook her head. "No, thanks," Jane said. "I'd better work on my science project."

"Me, too," Ben said quickly.

"I promised to help Jane," Annie added as Boris and Hilda went inside Hauntly Manor Inn.

"Since when do you want to do homework?" Jane asked Ben.

"Since never," Ben said. "I just wasn't hungry for raw meat."

"I like doing homework," Kilmer said. "In fact, I will hurry to finish my science project after our snack. Fang said he would help me."

Annie, Jane, and Ben watched Fang and Kilmer disappear inside the inn. Then Jane poked Ben in the arm. "We'd really better work on our science projects," she told Ben. "They're due on Monday."

Ben groaned as the three kids walked back to Ben and Annie's house. "I'd rather crack walnuts with my teeth," he told Jane. "There's something weird about kids who like to do homework."

"Nobody could be as weird as Fang," Jane said. "He's as hairy as my dad's hairbrush."

"He can't help having a lot of hair," Annie said. "Maybe it runs in his family."

"Maybe," Jane said, "if he comes from a family of hairy monsters that eat raw meat for snacks and howl like wolves."

"Very funny —" Annie started to say.

But she was interrupted by loud howling that sent cold chills up her spine.

# 4

## Serious Trouble

Annie huddled close to Jane. "There's only one thing that howls like that," Jane whispered. "A wolf!"

Annie gasped, but Ben laughed out loud. "There aren't any wolves in Bailey City," he told her.

Jane shook her head. "This is no ordinary wolf," she said. "I'm talking about a werewolf. And his name is Fang Hauntly."

Ben laughed so hard he sat down in the snow. "Then I'm the Abominable Snowman."

"Ben's right," Annie told her best friend. "Just because Kilmer's cousin is different, it doesn't mean he's a wolf. Besides, there are no such things as werewolves."

"But there are airheads," Ben said. "And you're the most famous of them all!" With

that, Ben tossed a snowball at Jane. Jane was too fast for him and she dodged the snowball. She quickly packed another one and it zoomed back to hit Ben on the head.

Ben jumped up and pointed at Jane. "You're asking for it," he warned her.

"And who is going to give it to me?" Jane said with a laugh.

"Me," Ben said, "with Kilmer and his cousin. We're going to challenge you to a rematch!" Ben stomped all the way to the Hauntlys' front door.

"You better not go in there," Jane warned. "That raw meat probably just made Fang hungrier. He'll gnaw your bones for dessert."

Ben ignored Jane and knocked on the front door of Hauntly Manor Inn.

Boris opened the front door and let Ben inside. Annie thought Boris' long cape made him look just like a vampire. Annie shivered. "If Fang really is a werewolf, Ben could be in trouble," she said. "Serious trouble."

"So?" Jane said.

"Ben is my brother," Annie told her. "I can't let him become a werewolf snack without trying to save him."

Jane shrugged. "He isn't my brother," she pointed out.

"But you're my best friend," Annie said. "So you have to help me."

Jane sighed and followed Annie back to Hauntly Manor. "I guess you're right. But if you ever tell anyone at school that I saved Ben, I'll deny it!"

"Don't worry," Annie said, knocking on the Hauntlys' door. "I won't tell anyone. Besides, they would never believe me!"

"So nice to see you again," Boris said in his Transylvanian accent as the door creaked open. "Won't you come in?"

The deep red button at Boris' throat looked like a giant drop of blood and his skin was white like the snow. The black cape swirled around Boris' legs, hiding his feet from view, as he led the girls deep into

the darkness of Hauntly Manor. Annie was sure Boris floated instead of walked.

Boris stopped in the doorway of the living room. The walls were painted bloodred and an ancient organ sat in the corner. A thick layer of dust covered everything. "Please, sit down while I whip up a special snack for you." Boris pointed to the velvet couch with legs that looked like claws.

Annie shook her head. "We just came to get Ben," she told Boris.

Boris nodded. "Ben went to find Kilmer and Fang."

"Is it okay if we look for him?" Jane asked.

"Of course," Boris told her. "But . . . do be careful."

"Be careful of what?" Annie asked. But Boris had already disappeared down the dark hallway.

"This place gives me the creeps," Jane said. "It reminds me of a scary movie."

Annie nodded. "I keep thinking something is going to jump out at me from a corner."

"Or grab my ankles," Jane said. Both girls looked at the giant claw feet of the couch and took a giant step away from it.

"Come on," Annie said. "If we're going to save Ben, we'd better hurry."

Together, the girls walked down the hall. Cobwebs hung from corners and a door at the end of the long hall slammed shut. Jane pointed. "Ben must be down there."

"What if he isn't?" Annie asked. "What if

Kilmer's flea-bitten cousin is waiting for us?"

Jane took a deep breath. "Just be ready to run." Together, the girls inched their way down the dark hallway. Step-by-step, closer they came, until they were halfway down the hall.

Annie and Jane never made it to the end of the hallway. As they passed a dark doorway, two hands reached out and grabbed their shoulders.

# 5

# Caught

Annie started to scream, but a hand slapped over her mouth. "Shh," a voice warned. "Don't let them hear you."

"Ben!" Annie hissed. "What are you doing? You scared us to death!"

"You shouldn't be hiding in Hauntly Manor," Jane told him.

Ben pulled Annie and Jane into the shadows. "I wasn't hiding," Ben said. "I was looking around. And I saw something . . . something unusual."

"Did you see Cousin Hauntly turning into a werewolf?" Jane asked.

Ben shook his head. "I haven't seen Kilmer and his cousin at all. But I did find Dr. Hauntly. She's cooking up something."

Annie and Jane knew all about the Hauntlys' strange treats. Boris and the rest of the Hauntlys had tried to give them skeleton knuckles and lizard tongues on Halloween.

Annie patted her brother on the arm. "Don't worry," she said. "You don't have to eat any of it."

"That's not the kind of cooking I'm talking about," Ben hissed.

"Then what are you jabbering about?" Jane asked.

Ben pulled them deeper into the dark hall. "Come with me and I'll show you."

"Sneaking around someone's house isn't polite," Annie said.

"Polite isn't in my vocabulary," Ben said, stopping in front of a closed door.

Gray mist oozed from beneath the door and when Jane sniffed she smelled something like cotton candy. "Whatever Dr. Hauntly is cooking, it smells good," Jane said.

"It's better than good," Ben said. "Look."

Ben slowly turned the doorknob to crack open the door. The three kids leaned close to peek into Dr. Hauntly's laboratory. Hilda Hauntly was a scientist at FATS, the Federal Aeronautics Technology Station. They knew she had a laboratory in Hauntly Manor, but they had never seen her working there.

Hilda stood in front of a long black counter. The counter was cluttered with test tubes and beakers. Some of the glass containers had green liquid, a few of them bubbled, and three of them had smoke rolling off the top. Hilda wasn't paying any attention to them. She was busy scribbling notes on a piece of paper. Then she carefully measured out a spoonful of creamy white stuff and dumped it into a metal bowl.

"Watch this," Ben whispered. "This is the good part."

Hilda flipped a switch and the bowl turned. It started out slow, then the bowl gained speed. Soon, the bowl twirled so fast that it looked blurry.

"What's she doing?" Annie asked softly.

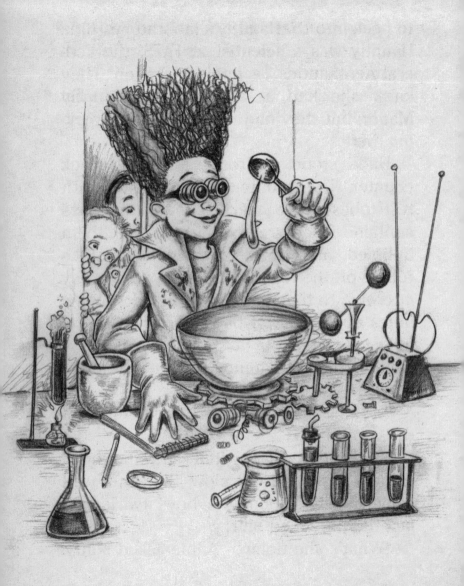

"Maybe she's making a Jane-Be-Gone potion," Ben joked, closing the door so Dr. Hauntly couldn't hear them.

Jane curled her fingers into a tight fist and held it in front of Ben's nose. "You better watch out or you'll be seeing stars! What she needs to make is an antiwerewolf formula."

"Don't start that crazy talk again," Ben said.

Annie opened her mouth to answer him, but she stopped when she heard a strange clicking. It sounded just like giant claws making their way across a wooden floor. And the claws were heading straight for them.

# 6
# Ready or Not

Jane ducked behind Ben. Annie jumped behind Jane. Ben stepped back and tripped over Jane. They all landed in a big pile.

"Why are you sitting on the floor?" Kilmer asked. He smiled down at his three neighbors. Next to Kilmer was his cousin, Fang.

Jane noticed Fang wasn't wearing any shoes. His feet were covered with thick black hair. Each toe ended in a long dirty-looking toenail.

"We're not sitting on the floor," Jane sputtered. "We fell."

Annie untangled herself and stood up. "You scared us," she explained. "We didn't expect to see you here."

Kilmer looked confused. "But I live here," he said.

Annie's face turned red and Jane looked down at her sneakers. Ben didn't bat an eye. "Of course you live here," he said. "Annie means we didn't expect you to find us so soon."

"But I wasn't looking for you," Kilmer said.

"How do you expect to win at hide-and-seek if you don't look for us?" Ben said.

"Hide-and-seek?" Kilmer asked.

"That's right!" Jane yelled. "Hide-and-seek. It's a game. We hide from you and you have to find us. Don't you want to play?"

Fang licked his lips. "How do you play?" he asked.

"It's simple," Annie said. "First, cover your eyes. While you count to one hundred, we hide. Then, you try to find us."

Fang shook his head. "That would be too easy," he said. "I could sniff you out in no time." He sniffed the air to prove his point.

"Besides," Kilmer said, "I want to work on my science project."

Ben rolled his eyes. "We can worry about that the night before it's due," he said.

"Do you mean you haven't even started your project?" Jane asked. "I began my research two weeks ago. It's all about the phases of the moon."

Fang scratched his chin with a long fingernail. "I know a lot about the moon's phases," he said. "I study the moon every night. Maybe I could help you."

"What a great idea!" Kilmer said. "You can bring your project over here and we'll work on them together. Annie can help us, too."

"But Ben hasn't even started his project," Annie argued.

"We can help him think of an idea," Kilmer said.

"All right!" Ben yelled.

Jane didn't cheer. She watched the gray mist oozing from under Dr. Hauntly's laboratory door and whispered, "I have a very bad feeling about this."

# 7

# Animal Control

Annie and Jane hurried down Dedman Street. Jane was carrying her poster about the moon. Annie looked up at Hauntly Manor. "I hope Ben is all right in there." The girls had left Ben at the inn while they went to get Jane's science project.

"Ben is the biggest monster on Dedman Street," Jane told Annie. "A werewolf would get sick just sniffing Ben's socks."

Annie giggled. "They're not white. They're not pink. But phe-ew, they sure do stink!"

Jane nodded. "Even monsters have certain standards!"

"Yeah, they can't stand Ben." Annie giggled. Annie stopped laughing when she saw a truck slowly making its way down Dedman Street. BAILEY CITY ANIMAL CONTROL was painted in big blue letters on the side. The

truck rolled to a stop in front of Hauntly Manor Inn.

Two men hopped out of the truck. One man carried a net. The other one carried a long stick with a rope looped on the end.

"Good afternoon, ladies," one of the men hollered from the road. "We're looking for a wild animal. You haven't seen one around, have you?"

Jane and Annie walked over to the truck. "What kind of wild animal?" Annie asked.

The man carrying the net grinned. "We got a strange report from this neighborhood," he said. "Some kook thinks he heard a wolf last night. Did you happen to see a big hairy wolf?"

"Not exactly," Jane said slowly.

The man with the stick nodded. "We didn't expect to find anything. Whoever heard of a wolf in the middle of Bailey City?" Both men laughed.

While the men laughed, Sparky tore around the corner of Hauntly Manor. Sparky came close to the men, skidded to a stop, and arched her back. She laid her ears flat against her head and hissed. Then she jumped onto the porch and sprang onto a window screen.

"That cat looks like it's being chased by a wolf," the man with the net said.

The other man threw his stick back into the truck. "There's nothing here but a crazy cat," he said. "Let's get out of here."

"Don't worry, girls," the man with the net said. "If we hear any more complaints we'll be back. If there is a wolf, we'll catch it!" The two men from the Bailey City Animal Control Department climbed back into their truck and roared off down Dedman Street.

Annie looked at Jane. Jane looked at Annie. Then they both slowly turned around to look at Hauntly Manor.

# 8

## Spider Names

"We've got to do something," Jane told Annie as they walked up the Hauntlys' front walk. "Those men were talking about a wolf and I know exactly who that wolf is."

The two girls jumped when a growl came from above them. Fang stood on the porch, glaring down at the two girls. He didn't wear a coat, even though it was freezing. Annie noticed that Fang was still barefoot. She stared at his feet and shivered, but it wasn't from the cold. She was sure that Fang's feet were hairier than before.

"Is something wrong?" Fang asked.

"We were just talking about my science project," Jane lied.

Fang smiled. "I've been waiting for you. I

cannot wait to get started. Follow me," he said, disappearing through the door.

Jane and Annie slowly climbed the creaking porch steps of Hauntly Manor. "I don't want to go in there," Annie whispered to Jane. "What if Fang gets us?"

"Werewolves only eat people at night," Jane whispered, "when there's a full moon. We don't have to worry." She held up her poster for Annie to see. "The next full moon isn't until tomorrow night."

"It's about time," Ben said when the girls finally made it to Kilmer's bedroom.

Kilmer's bedroom wasn't like most fourth-graders' rooms. It looked like the darkest night, even though it was bright day outside. That's because the walls and ceiling were painted black. A shiny metal table was pushed up against one wall, and a jumble of big wires trailed down from the ceiling. Kilmer didn't even have a regular bed. Instead, there were black blankets and pillows piled on a wooden slab.

Ben pointed to the metal table. "Wait

until you see Kilmer's project," he told the girls.

Annie and Jane looked at three glass boxes filled with lacy webs. In each box, a giant hairy spider was busy spinning more.

"I'm studying the patterns in webs made by different spiders," Kilmer explained. Jane put her project next to Kilmer's. Then she took three steps back.

"Are you sure they're safe?" Annie asked.

Kilmer looked at the spiders in their glass boxes. "Elvira, Winifred, and Minerva wouldn't hurt anything," he said.

"You named your spiders?" Jane asked.

Kilmer blinked. "Of course," he said. "Doesn't everybody?"

"You've done a lot of work," Ben admitted. "I'll never get my project done."

"You should have started a long time ago," Annie lectured.

"Perhaps you would like to spend the

night," Fang suggested. "Then I could help you. After all, there is plenty of room at the inn."

Annie shivered, Jane gulped, but Ben grinned. "That would be perfect," he said. "I came up with a brilliant idea. I'm going to convince your mother to cook up a science project for me."

Kilmer shook his head. "Do not count on it. My mother's experiments are not always what they seem."

"That would be cheating," Annie said. "You have to do your own project just like Jane and Kilmer."

"I will help you," Fang said.

"We will help each other," Kilmer said. "Let us go ask Father if everyone can stay the night."

As soon as Kilmer and Fang left the room, Jane grabbed Ben's arm. "You're not really spending the night here, are you?" she asked him.

Ben grinned. "Of course I am," he said. "I need Fang's help on my report. The two of you will spend the night, too. Unless you're chicken."

"I'm not scared," Jane said quickly.

"Well," Annie said, "I am. I don't want to stay in this creepy place with a werewolf."

"You can't really believe Fang is a were-wolf," Ben said with a laugh.

Annie shrugged. "He does have a lot of hair," she said.

"Teenagers are like that," Ben said. "Just wait until I'm a few years older. I'll have lots of hair, too."

"What about his voice?" Jane argued. "Sometimes it sounds just like a growl."

"It's normal for teenagers' voices to change," Ben said.

"Is it normal for the Bailey City Animal Control to be looking for wolves on Ded-man Street?" Jane asked. She told Ben what happened when they left to get her science project.

"Aren't you a little scared?" Annie asked Ben.

"I'm not afraid of Fang," Ben said, "be-

cause he's not a werewolf. He's just a hairy teenager from Transylvania. I'll prove it by sleeping in the same room with him tonight."

"We hope you're right," Annie said. "Because if you're not, you may be sleeping with a werewolf!"

# 9
# Late Night

"I can't believe you talked me into spending the night in a haunted house," Annie complained as the kids came back to the Hauntlys' after eating dinner at their own houses.

"I was hoping my mother would say no," Jane admitted.

Ben lifted the heavy door knocker and shook his head. "You guys are wimps. It'll be exciting. We'll have something to brag about at school."

"I just hope we'll be alive to brag," Annie said right before the huge wooden door creaked open and Kilmer ushered them inside.

The kids stayed up late working on their projects. Kilmer carefully drew pictures of the different webs that Elvira, Winifred, and

Minerva made. Fang helped Annie and Jane make a calendar showing the phases of the moon. Ben sat on the floor and tossed a small rubber ball against the wall.

"I can't think of anything to do," Ben complained.

"You're just scared of hard work," Annie told her brother.

"I'm not scared of anything," Ben snapped.

"Yes, you are," Jane blurted. "You're a big chicken when it comes to working."

Fang tilted his head back and howled with laughter. "Jane just gave me a delicious idea for your project," Fang told Ben.

"What is it?" Ben asked hopefully.

Fang grinned so big his yellow canine teeth showed. "I have some chicken bones that you could put back together to make a chicken skeleton."

"Where did you get those?" Jane asked.

Fang smiled and licked his lips. "Oh, I just collected them. Ben could label the bones and even make a poster showing the parts."

"Will you help me?" Ben asked.

"I'd be happy to help," Fang said. "We'll start now."

Fang hurried from the room, but he soon returned with a glass bowl that reminded Jane of her grandmother's candy dish. Only, Fang's bowl didn't hold chocolates. It was filled with bones. Fang licked his lips when he dumped the bleached bones onto the floor. When he helped Ben sort them, Fang's stomach growled.

Ben and Fang worked very late. Finally, Ben yawned. "I'm so tired, I could sleep in the middle of a bullfight," he said.

Fang didn't look tired at all. He didn't say a word when Ben and Kilmer curled up on the wooden slab and went to sleep.

The girls had already crawled into the strange iron beds in the next room. But no matter how hard they tried, Annie and Jane couldn't sleep. At first, they thought they heard chains rattling in the attic. Then

there was a loud bang as if someone had slammed a door. Outside, the wind whipped through the branches of the dead tree in the Hauntlys' front yard.

Annie pulled a pillow over her head, but that didn't help. The wind blew even harder, and she was sure she heard something besides the wind.

"Ahh-ewwwww."

"Did you hear that?" Annie whispered.

"It's the wind," Jane said, but she didn't sound very sure.

"Ahh-ewwww!"

Annie sat up. "There it is again," she whispered.

Jane nodded. "I hear it, too," she said.

"Ahh-ewww. Ahh-EWWWW. AHH-EWW-WWWW."

Annie grabbed Jane's hand. "Something outside is howling."

"Let's find out what it is," Jane said, jumping out of bed to look out the window. It was nearly midnight, but bright moonlight shone on the Hauntlys' backyard.

"Look," Jane hissed, "on top of that old shed."

Annie gasped. A huge creature was perched on top of the shed. It was definitely bigger than Sparky. It was even bigger than a dog. As the two girls stared, the animal lifted its head to look at the moon and howled a lonely cry.

"We're in big trouble," Annie whimpered. "It's a werewolf and he's howling at the full moon."

"The moon isn't quite full," Jane whispered. "I learned that when it's almost full it's called a gibbous moon. That must be why he is howling. He wants a full moon."

"I have to make sure Ben is okay," Annie said. "And you're coming with me."

The girls pulled their blankets tight around them and crept down the hallway to Kilmer's bedroom. Annie turned the doorknob until the door slowly creaked open. Jane flipped the switch, flooding Kilmer's room with light.

Kilmer and Ben were sleeping on the

wooden slab. When the light came on, Ben sat up and blinked. "What's the big idea?" Ben asked, rubbing his eyes. "You look like two ghosts that got lost in the dark."

Kilmer yawned and shook his head. "No, they don't," he said. "They look nothing like ghosts." He lay back down and went to sleep again.

Annie whispered to Ben. "We heard something," she told Ben. "We were worried about you."

"There's nothing to worry about," Ben told the girls. "We're all sleeping like babies."

"Oh, yeah?" Jane asked. "If that's true, then where is Fang?"

Annie, Jane, and Ben looked around the room. Kilmer was snoring on his slab, but Fang was nowhere to be found.

Just then a dark shadow fell across the room. Slowly, Jane and Annie turned around.

Fang stood in the doorway, and he didn't look happy.

# 10

## Midnight Snacks

The next morning, Hilda Hauntly placed a tray on the big table. Jane, Annie, and Ben stared at the pile of bloody rare meat.

"Mmmm," Fang growled. "My favorite breakfast." He stuck his fork into a big piece of meat still attached to a bone and plopped it on his plate. He picked up the bone and started sucking off the meat.

Ben looked at Fang. "I hope you're not still mad about last night," Ben said. "Remember, you promised to help me finish my project."

Fang stopped gnawing on his bone. "I'm not mad, but you weren't supposed to be out of your room," Fang told Annie and Jane. "I told Aunt Hilda and Uncle Boris I would make sure you went to bed early."

"We're sorry," Annie said with a gulp.

"But," Jane said, looking Fang straight in the eyes, "you weren't in bed, either. Where were you?"

Before he answered, Fang picked at a piece of meat stuck between his front teeth with one of his long fingernails. "I was just having a little midnight snack," he finally said.

"Then you would have heard it, too," Annie said.

"Heard what?" Kilmer asked.

"They thought they heard howling," Ben said with a laugh.

Kilmer and Fang didn't laugh. Instead, they looked down at their breakfast plates.

"You'll still help me finish my project, won't you?" Ben asked Fang again.

Fang nodded. "I'll help," he said.

Boris smiled at Annie, Ben, and Jane. "Aren't you hungry this morning?" he asked. "Perhaps you would prefer eggs."

Ben grinned. "Eggs sound good."

Boris grabbed a tray of yellow blobs and

held it out to Ben. "I make a mean scrambled rat snake egg," he said.

Annie gulped and Jane's face looked as pale as milk.

"Actually," Ben said, "I'm not really that hungry."

"We should get home," Annie added.

"But you haven't eaten," Kilmer said. "A good breakfast is the most important meal of the day."

Annie, Jane, and Ben looked at the gooey rat snake eggs and raw meat. "We'll grab a bite a little later," Annie said. "We should really be going home now. Thanks for letting us spend the night."

"We'll be back later to work on our science projects," Ben said.

"After lunch," Jane added as she took one last look at the bloody meat.

Annie, Jane, and Ben rushed outside. Jane stopped her friends before they went too far. "Now we know for sure," she said. "Fang is one hundred percent werewolf and just two percent teenager."

"You better quit calling my friend names," Ben said.

"Didn't you notice that Fang is the hairiest teenager on the planet?" Jane said. "And he's getting even hairier."

"That would describe any teenager," Ben said. "Fang is really a great guy. Most teenagers wouldn't bother spitting on our shoes. But Fang helped us. I wouldn't even have a science project if it wasn't for him."

Annie nodded. "Ben's right. I like Fang, too. He really is nice and he helped you get the phases of the moon right," she told Jane.

Jane shrugged. "That's because most teenagers aren't werewolves, so they aren't experts on the moon and bones."

"I don't care if Fang is King Kong," Ben said. "He's smart and he helped us with our projects. As far as I'm concerned, Fang can stay here and YOU can fly to Transylvania."

"Even if it means living next door to a hairy werewolf?" Jane asked.

"It doesn't matter what he looks like," Annie told her. "Fang is our friend."

"What about the rest of the neighbors?" Jane asked. "People are complaining about Fang's howling. If he keeps it up, the Animal Control guys will come back. And one of these days, they'll catch Fang."

"Fang is pretty hairy and someone might mistake him for a werewolf when he's kidding around howling," Ben admitted. "We have to help him. I bet Kilmer will help, too."

"I'm sure Kilmer will help us if we ask," Annie said.

"What can we do?" Jane asked.

"We'd better think of something fast," Annie said.

"Don't worry," Ben said. "I have a plan."

# 11

# Werewolf Rescue

"Do you think this will work?" Annie asked.

"Of course," Ben said. It was just starting to get dark and Ben, Annie, and Jane were waiting in front of Hauntly Manor.

Annie shivered in the cold wind. "I hope so," she told Ben.

Jane tossed a snowball in the air. "We're supposed to be pretending to have a snowball fight, remember?"

Annie nodded and reached down to make a snowball. Just then, the back door to Hauntly Manor slammed. Heavy footsteps came straight toward them. Annie was ready to run when a familiar face peeped around the corner of the inn. Kilmer smiled at his three friends. "Are you ready?" Kilmer asked.

"Ready and waiting," Ben said.

"Are you sure Fang is out of sight?" Jane asked.

Kilmer nodded. "He's busy gnawing on a roasted boar's head in the basement," he told them. "I locked the door, just to be sure. Do you really think this will work?"

"It's got to work," Ben said. "Fang's life depends on it."

"Then I better get ready," Kilmer said. He disappeared behind Hauntly Manor just as the huge white Animal Control truck squeaked to a stop in front of the inn. The two men in white jumped out. One man had a net and the other had a gun.

"Oh, my gosh," Annie whispered. "Are they going to kill Fang?"

Jane patted Annie's shoulder. "Don't worry, that's a tranquilizer gun. It just puts animals to sleep."

The man with a net waved at them. "Seems like more of your neighbors heard that animal last night," he said.

"What animal?" Ben asked.

67

The two men shrugged. "Whatever it is, it must be big," the net man said. "The Animal Control office got fifteen calls last night. All around midnight."

"What are you going to do with this animal if you find it?" Ben asked.

The net man shrugged. "Same thing we always do. Put it in a little cage until someone finds a zoo for it."

"Unless it's too wild," the other man said.

"Then what happens?" Annie asked.

The man shrugged. "I'd rather not say. But when a big wild animal gets used to living around humans, they become dangerous. We can't let them wander loose."

"So," the first man asked, "have you kids seen any signs of a wild animal?"

"Well," Ben said. "Maybe back in the toolshed."

The two men ran toward the shed. When they ran into the shed, they got the surprise of their lives. Buckets of dust and cobwebs fell right on their heads. The men were covered with the sticky webs from Elvira, Winifred, and Minerva.

"Help!" the men screamed. "Get us out of this mess."

Annie, Ben, and Jane ran over to the men.

"What is going on here?" one of the men said, wiping dust off his head.

"Nothing but a little kids' stuff," Jane explained. "We're sorry about the mess. But we'll make you a deal. If we promise to make sure the howling stops, will you leave Hauntly Manor alone?"

One of the men shrieked and pulled a big black spider out of his hair. "Listen kid, I never want to see this place again as long as I live. You have a deal." Both men ran out of the backyard, the wheels of their truck screeching as they sped away.

Kilmer came over to his friends after the men had gone. Ben slapped Kilmer on his back. Kilmer reached down and picked up Minerva. "Good girl," Kilmer told the spider.

69

"Now our only problem is how to keep Fang from howling at the moon," Jane said.

"You do not have to worry about that," Kilmer said. "Fang is going home tomorrow. Right now, I should get Minerva back in her container before she catches cold." Kilmer cuddled his pet spider and walked into Hauntly Manor Inn.

"Whew!" Annie said. "What a night."

"I am going to miss Fang," Ben said. "He's a nice guy."

"A nice werewolf," Jane corrected, "and we're safe from werewolves now that he's leaving."

"You forgot one thing," Ben said. "If Fang can fly out, that means . . ."

"More monsters can fly in," Jane finished.

"What could be weirder than having a werewolf next door?" Annie asked.

Jane shivered. "I don't know, but I have a feeling we're going to find out."

# About the Authors

Marcia Thornton Jones and Debbie Dadey like to write about monsters. Their first series with Scholastic, **The Adventures of the Bailey School Kids,** has many characters who are *monsterously* funny. Now with the Hauntly family, Marcia and Debbie are in monster heaven!

Marcia and Debbie both used to live in Lexington, Kentucky. They were teachers at the same elementary school. When Debbie moved to Aurora, Illinois, she and Marcia had to change how they worked together. These authors now create monster books long-distance. They play hot potato with their stories, passing them back and forth by computer.

# About the Illustrator

John Steven Gurney is the illustrator of both **The Bailey City Monsters** and **The Adventures of the Bailey School Kids.** He uses real people in his own neighborhood as models when he draws the characters in Bailey City. John has illustrated many books for young readers. He lives in Vermont with his wife and two children.